WHAT THE WHAT?

by Kirsten Maye

PSS!
PRICE STERN SLOAN
An Imprint of Penguin Group (USA) LLC

D1384373

PRICE STERN SLOAN
Published by the Penguin Group
Penguin Group (USA) LLC
375 Hudson Street
New York, New York 10014, USA

USA I Canada I UK I Ireland I Australia I New Zealand I India I South Africa I China

penguin.com
A Penguin Random House Company

Penguin supports copyright. Copyright fuels creativity, encourages diverse voices, promotes free speech, and creates a vibrant culture.
Thank you for buying an authorized edition of this book and for complying with copyright laws by not reproducing, scanning, or distributing
any part of it in any form without permission. You are supporting writers and allowing Penguin to continue to publish books for every reader.

ADVENTURE TIME, CARTOON NETWORK, the logos, and all related characters and
elements are trademarks of and © Cartoon Network. (s13)

Published in 2013 by Price Stern Sloan, a division of Penguin Young Readers Group, 345 Hudson Street,
New York, New York 10014. *PSS!* is a registered trademark of Penguin Group (USA) LLC.
Printed in the U.S.A.

ISBN 978-0-8431-8018-3   10 9 8 7 6 5 4 3 2 1

The insides of Jake smell like VANILLA, due to a wizard's curse.

STONESKIN POTION GIVES YOUR BODY THE POWER TO GROW ARMOR.
FARTS CAN STOP FRUIT WITCHES.

Ooo holds an ICE CREAM MARATHON, which involves eating a **LOT** of ice cream.

Playing MOZART on the viola ATTRACTS SNAKES.

Marauders drink squid ink.

An arena is an enclosed space for entertainment—like the gladiator fights. The word derives from the Latin harena, a particularly fine sand that was used to absorb BLOOD.

EVERYTHING BRAINLESS LIKES MUSIC.

The Enchiridion is a book meant only for heroes whose HEARTS ARE RIGHTEOUS.

To cure the meat of a HAMMERHEAD SHARK, hang it upside down by the tail.

BEARS LIKE TO PARTY.

WHEN STARTLED, THE INCHWORM STOPS, REARS STRAIGHT UP, AND STANDS STILL.
Princess Bubblegum participates in the Whistling Choir Deathmatch Championship.

THE GLASSES OF NERDOCON WILL SHOW YOU THAT EVERYTHING

SMALL IS JUST A SMALL VERSION OF SOMETHING BIG.

IT'S BEST TO STAY INSIDE DURING KNIFE STORMS.

The annual Technology Fair is held in VEGGIE VILLAGE.

CINNAMON BUN WILL EAT ANYTHING, EVEN ZOMBIE FLESH.

Finn wears tighty-whities.

THERE ARE SOMEWHERE BETWEEN 21 TO 23 BERRIES IN THE BODY OF A WILDBERRY PRINCESS.

FOR MOST PEOPLE, WHISTLING IS EASIER IF YOUR LIPS ARE MOIST. TRY LICKING YOUR LIPS, AND MAYBE TAKING A SIP OF WATER.

THE LUTE IS A STRINGED INSTRUMENT THAT WAS VERY POPULAR IN THE RENAISSANCE. IT WAS TRADITIONALLY PLAYED TO WOO LADIES.

Birds chew up food and then barf it back up to feed their babies.

The Ice King's drum kit says #1 BABE on it.

A gladiator was an armed combatant who entertained audiences in violent confrontations with other gladiators, most often in a fight to the

DEATH.

POURING SALT ON SLUGS CAN HURT THEM —IT CAUSES THEM TO DRY OUT.

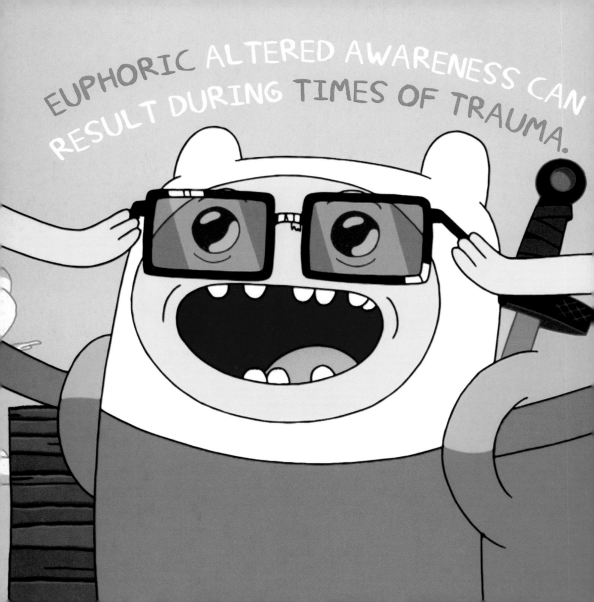

A NONFUNCTIONING DECORPSINATOR SERUM CREATES **ZOMBIES.**

APPLE JUICE ALWAYS MAKES FINN FEEL BETTER AFTER HE LOSES A GAME OF BUG BATTLE.

IN IMAGINATION LAND, THERE'S AN IMAGINATION MAN.

Soul food won't bring back your soul.

Flakes from the Ice King's beard can cause infections among Candy People.

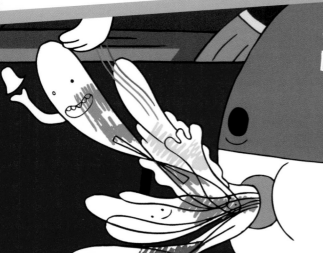

The Clambulance had the best clams in town

THE
CLAMBULANCE
*
BEST
CLAMS IN
TOWN

JIGGLERS CAN EAT PICTURES OF FOOD.

THE BEST TIME OF DAY BOTH FOR HANGING OUT WITH GIRLFRIENDS AND FOR FIGHTING SHARKS AND CATS IS 4 P.M.

HAWKS EAT ...
UH ... GENTLY
CARRY AWAY
BUNNIES.

NINJUTSU IS A MARTIAL ART —THOSE WHO PRACTICE THIS ART ARE CALLED NINJAS.

PRINCESS BUBBLEGUM'S FIRST NAME IS BONNIBEL.

THERE ARE 12 BARS ON THE PRINCESS CAGE IN THE ICE KING'S BEDROOM.

RESULTS...

BLASTRONAUT
-#1 SOLUTION
FOR ALL
HITMAN
PROBLEMS
$99.95!
PLACE ORDER

A Blastronaut costs $99.95.

IN THE VIDEO GAME *GUARDIANS OF SUNSHINE*, THE GOAL OF THE GAME IS TO PROTECT THE SUN.

IN THE GAME YOU CAN:

Defeat Bouncy Bee for 500 points.

Defeat Hunny Bunny for 800 points.

Defeat Sleepy Sam to win the game.

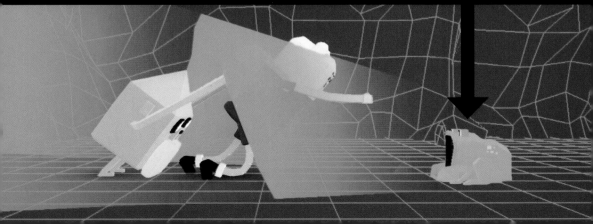

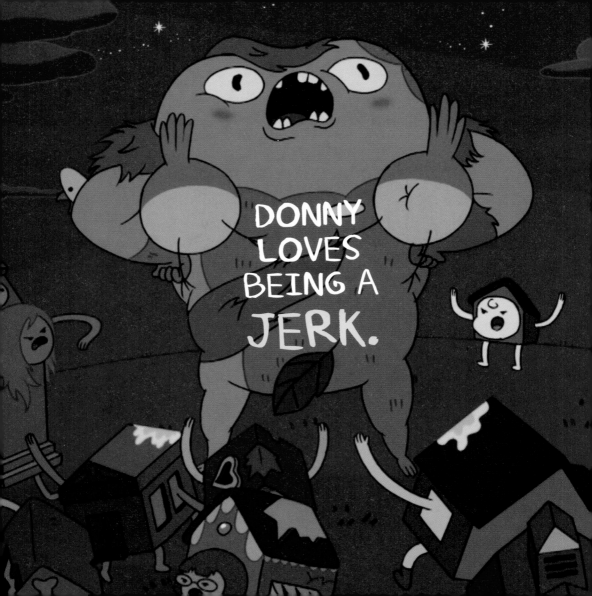

Wolves like to eat watermelon, pumpkin, and DEAD HORSES.

PRINCESS BUBBLEGUM
RIDES ON A BIRD
CALLED THE **MORROW.**

BANANA MAN LIVES
IN A GEODESIC DOME.

There is a Royal Day of Apology the day after everyone recovers from a ZOMBIE outbreak.

996 years ago Marceline and Simon hung out, when he was 47 years old and she was 7 years old.

Jake likes chamomile tea.

IN THE CRYSTAL DIMENSION, TREE TRUNKS BECAME QUARTZION THE CRYSTAL QUEEN.

AN ICEPEDE HAS 18 LEGS.

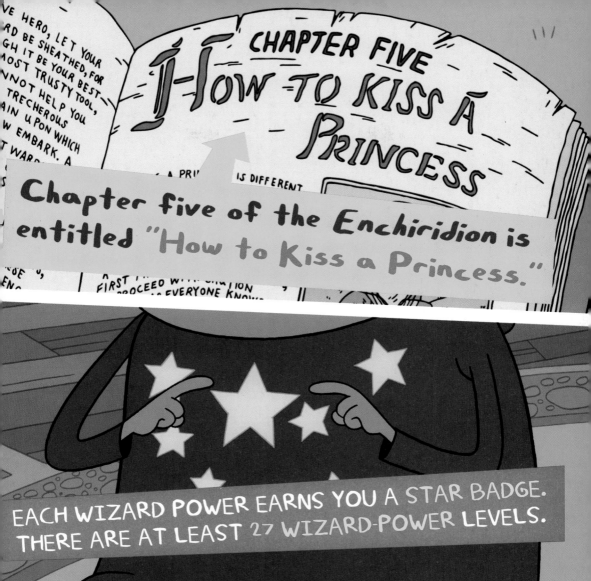

BEWARE MAGIC BEANS—THEY GROW GIANT BEANSTALKS WITH GIANT BEANS THAT HAVE WEIRD STUFF INSIDE LIKE PIGS, MAGIC WANDS, AND ICE CREAM.

When you're depressed,
you do nothing.

SIMON PETRIKOV WAS A FAN OF

THE TELEVISION SHOW *CHEERS.*

Banana Man exercises in his living room with a video.

WHY-WOLVES **LIKE TO ATTACK CUTE** LITTLE HOUSE PEOPLE.

WHEN TRAVELING BY BALLOON, HIDE YOUR WALLET. BALLOONS ARE KNOWN PICKPOCKETS.

THE MOST POPULAR TYPE OF PIE IN OOO IS APPLE PIE MADE BY TREE TRUNKS.

An asteroid was on a collision course with the Wizard Village for 847 years!

CHIONOPHOBIA IS A FEAR OF SNOW.

In history, there were Rainicorn-Dog wars that lasted for thousands of years, during which they fought over territory in the Crystal Dimension.

THE CUTE KING AND HIS LEGION OF CUTIES TRY TO BE EVIL . . . BUT THEY TEND TO **EXPLODE WHILE RUNNING.**

A GOOD ROOF PARTY NEEDS CHIPS, DIP, AND A COOLER FULL OF DRINKS.

Rats can win the Royal Medal for Heroic Bravery.

BANANA
MAN BUILT
A ROCKET!

WHISTLING CAN ATTRACT
BABY JIGGLERS.

Snow Golems and Fire Wolves are natural enemies.

A GROUP OF BEAVERS IS CALLED A COLONY.

THERE IS A WEEKLY PROMCOMING

DANCE HELD IN LUMPY SPACE.

No. 25 Blood Drive is the home of the ghosts named Wendy, Booboo, and Georgie.

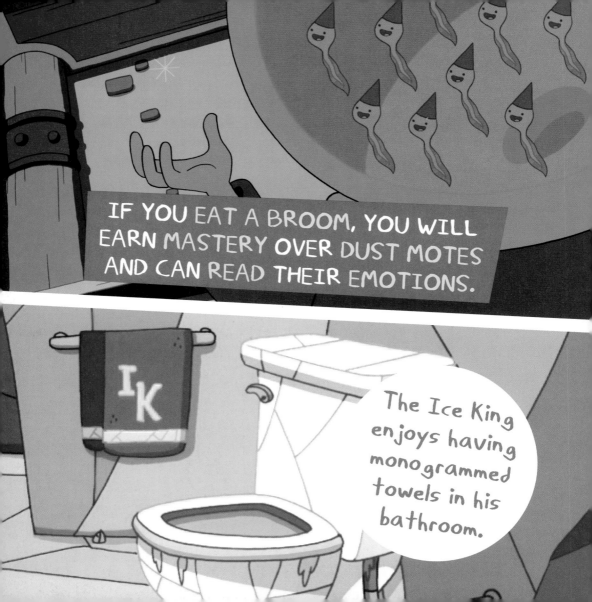

MARCELINE IS MORE THAN 1,000 YEARS OLD.

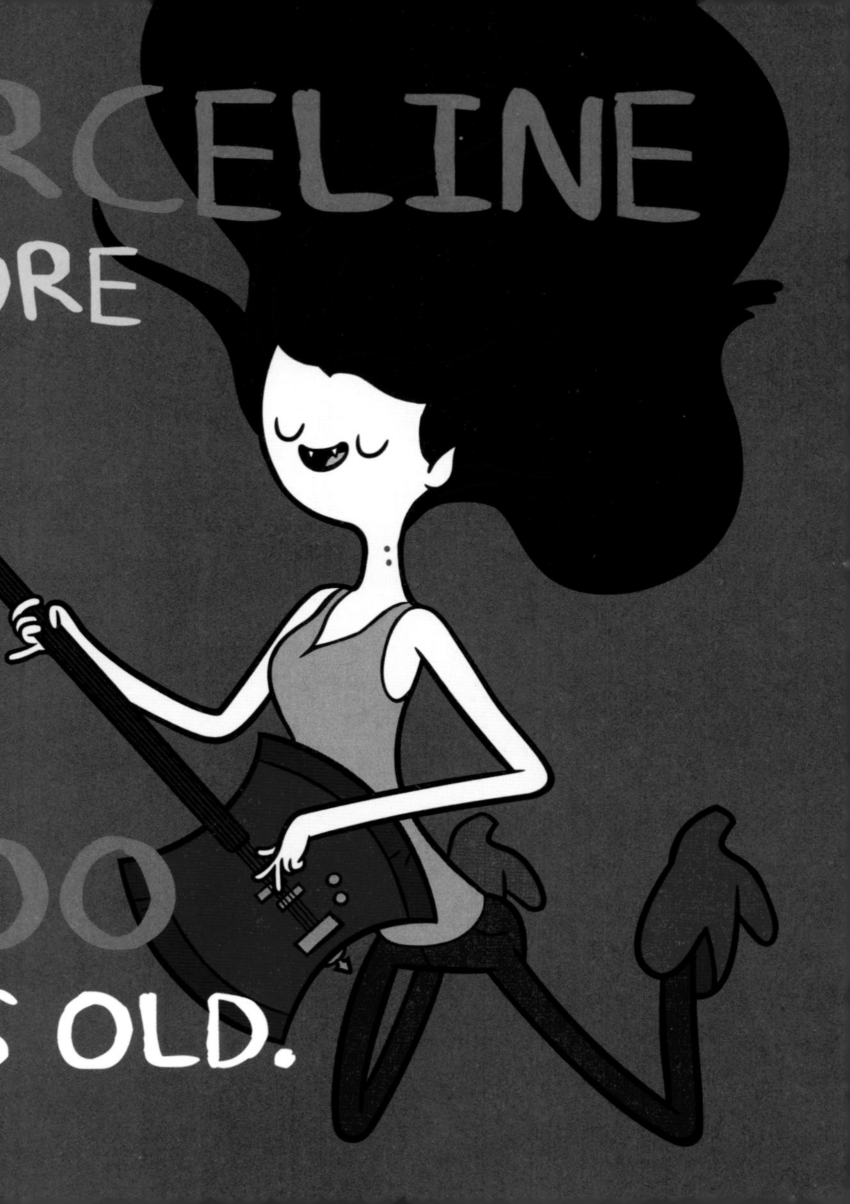

A good story has excitement, romance, suspense, and a happy ending.

(AND A FIGHT.)

romance
fight
suspense
Happy End

TRUTH OR DARE IS A FUN GAME TO PLAY AT SLUMBER PARTIES.

LUB GLUBS LOOK LIKE POOL TOYS ...BUT THEY ARE REALLY EVIL CREATURES WITH BIG NASTY TEETH.

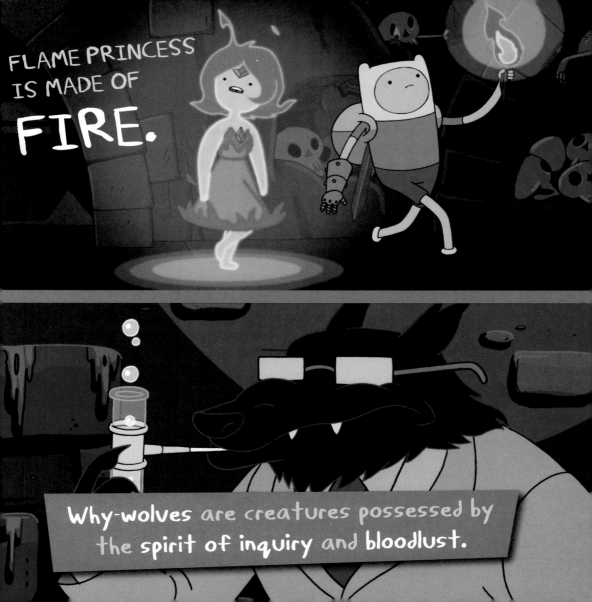

MAZES can have **MORE THAN ONE PATH** through them.

RAINICORN BODIES INTERCEPT BOUNCING LIGHT AND DANCE ON IT — WHICH MAKES IT LOOK LIKE THEY ARE FLYING.

CYCLOPS TEARS CAN CURE ANY INJURY.

LASERS ARE MUCH EASIER ON THE STOMACH THAN **FIREWORKS.**

CLOWN NURSES ARE **FUNNY.**

The smallest origami crane ever was made from a 0.1 millimeter square piece of paper.

IN ONE ACRE OF LAND, THERE CAN BE MORE THAN 1,000,000 EARTHWORMS.

JAKE DOESN'T KNOW WHAT POISON SMELLS LIKE.

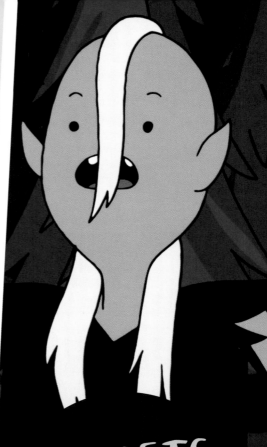

ASH GETS HUNGIES AT 8 O'CLOCK.

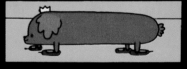

THERE'S STILL CELL PHONE RECEPTION
IN OOO, UNLESS A **LOT OF PRINCESSES**
ARE CALLING EACH OTHER.

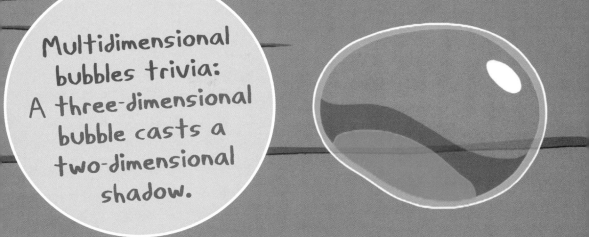

Multidimensional bubbles trivia: A three-dimensional bubble casts a two-dimensional shadow.

SPIDERWEBS OVER 80 FEET ACROSS HAVE BEEN FOUND IN THE WILD.

BMO plays soccer.

EVERY 100 YEARS THE TREE OF BLIGHT SPEWS EVIL SPORES ACROSS THE LAND.

THE MOAT AROUND THE CANDY CASTLE IS FILLED WITH

THESE CLUES WILL NOT HELP YOU SOLVE A MYSTERY ON A TRAIN:

EGGS, FISH, AND CABBAGE

RECEIPT FROM AN EARLIER TRAIN RIDE ON ANOTHER TRAIN

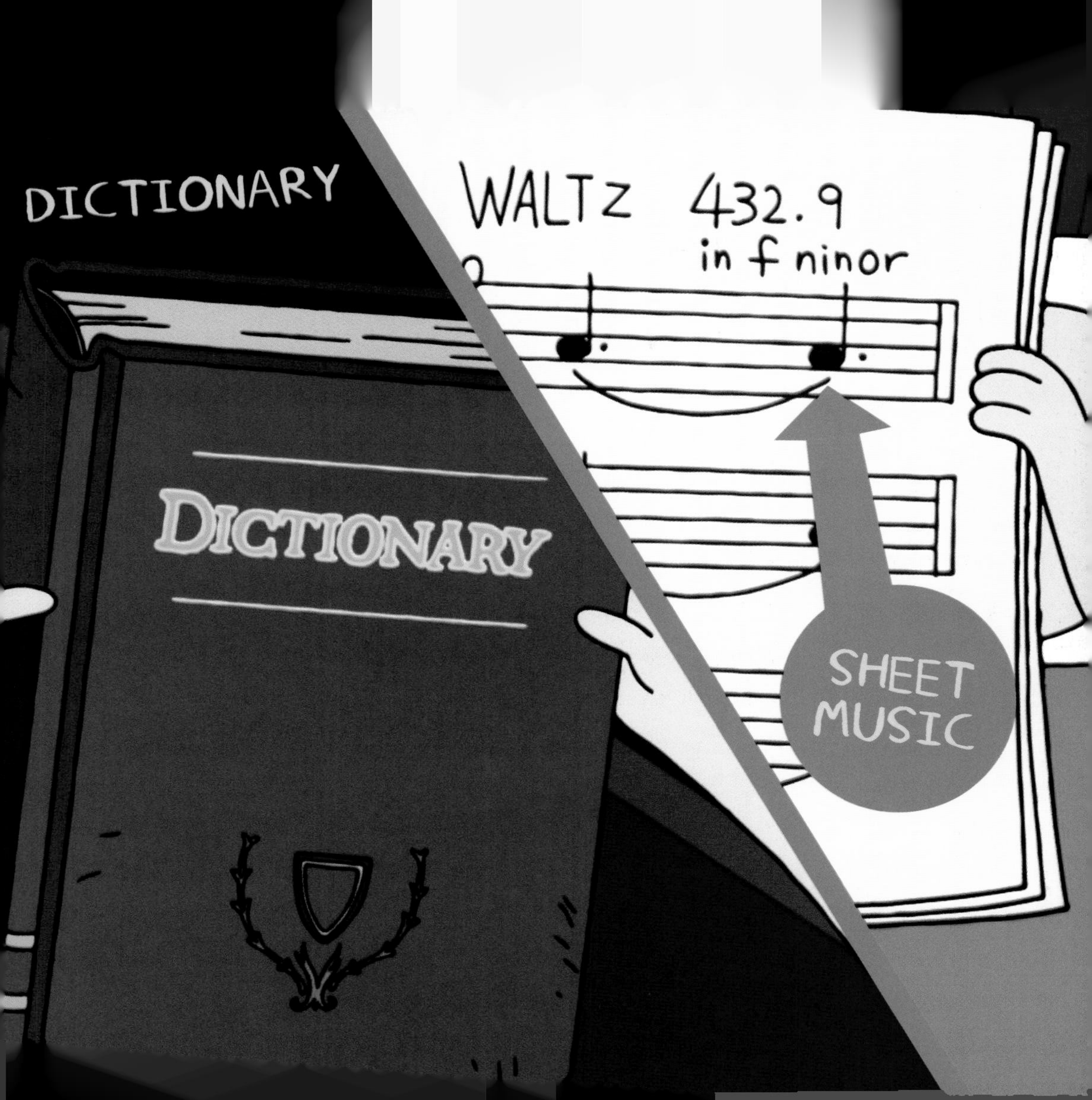
DICTIONARY
DICTIONARY
WALTz 432.9
in f ninor
SHEET MUSIC

Ethel and Bob are the names of Lady Rainicorn's parents.

A SCORCHER'S RECEIPT SAYS:

Echos of past events
nudge the tiller on
my present course
I await it's reflection
in the future

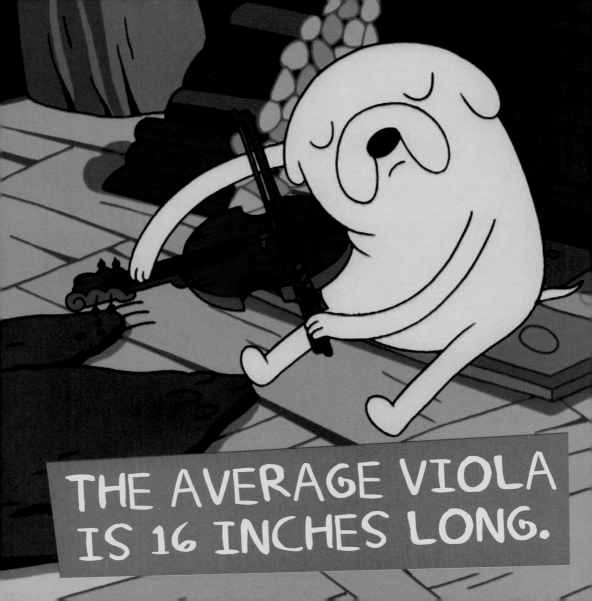

THE AVERAGE VIOLA IS 16 INCHES LONG.

EXTREME BLUSHING IS OFTEN ACCOMPANIED BY EXCESSIVE SWEATING.

If you offend the inhabitants of the forest, you will be subjected to the Rite of Forest Justice, wherein you must become one with the soil.

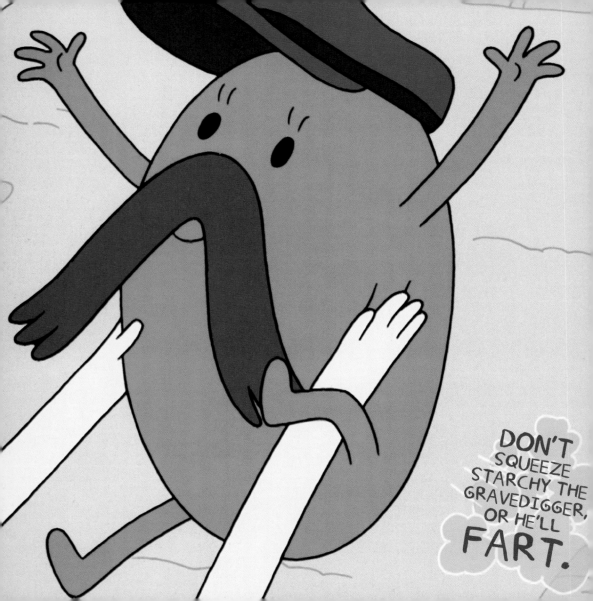

DON'T SQUEEZE STARCHY THE GRAVEDIGGER, OR HE'LL FART.

THERE'S A SECRET DOOR TO THE CANDY CASTLE DUNGEON.

Marceline's dad is deathless— you can't KILL HIM.

The goblins' king rules by *The Book of Royal Rules*, which contains 623 royal rules. They were established in Moon Year 16.

JAKE IS AFRAID OF REAL EMOTION.

RAINICORNICOPIA: AN UNABRIDGED HISTORY OF THE RAINICORNS

is a book too long to read.

MARCELINE PICKS HER NOSE.

Drinking the juice of the Elder Toad can cause hallucinations and/or forgetfulness.

THE INSIDES OF A NIGHTOSPHERE HALF MONSTER DEMON ARE HABITABLE.

PRINCESS BUBBLEGUM
INVENTED LIQUID
PYROTECHNICS.

HUG WOLVES HAVE HEART-SHAPED PAWS.

The Bestiarium Vocabulum (Beast Compendium) ((Animal Book)) lists Hug Wolves as "a subset of Wolfmen which roam the countryside with a fervid hug lust."

The Bestiarium Vocabulum (Beast Compendium) ((Animal Book)) also notes, "to become a Hug Wolf, one must be hugged by an Alpha Hug Wolf on the night of a full moon."

TWO HUG WOLVES CAN HUG IT OUT TO BREAK THE CURSE.

THE ICE KING HAS
A SET OF
NESTING
DOLLS.

NEPTR was hiding for a game of hide-and-seek for 15 months, 4 days, and 9 hours.

THREE IS MORE THAN ONE.

The Flame King's favorite thing in the world was a koala bear ... until he didn't like them anymore.

HUNSON ABADEER WEARS BOXERS.

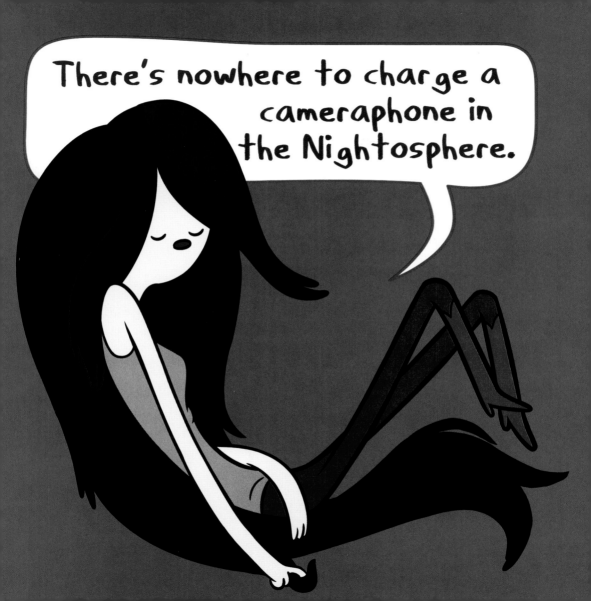

Stickers come in a variety of types, including rainbow, hologram, scratch-and-sniff, and foil.

NINJAS TRADITIONALLY SERVE AS SPIES. THEY SNEAK AROUND AND LEAVE NO TRACE THAT THEY WERE THERE.

RAINICORNS USED TO EAT HUMANS, BUT SINCE HUMANS BECAME MOSTLY EXTINCT, RAINICORNS NOW EAT SOY HUMANS.

MINSTRELS ARE MUSICIANS AND ENTERTAINERS WHO RECITE LONG EPIC POEMS OR SING BALLADS TELLING ABOUT COURTLY LOVE OR HEROIC TALES.

IT'S PROBABLY SOMETHING'S HOUSE.

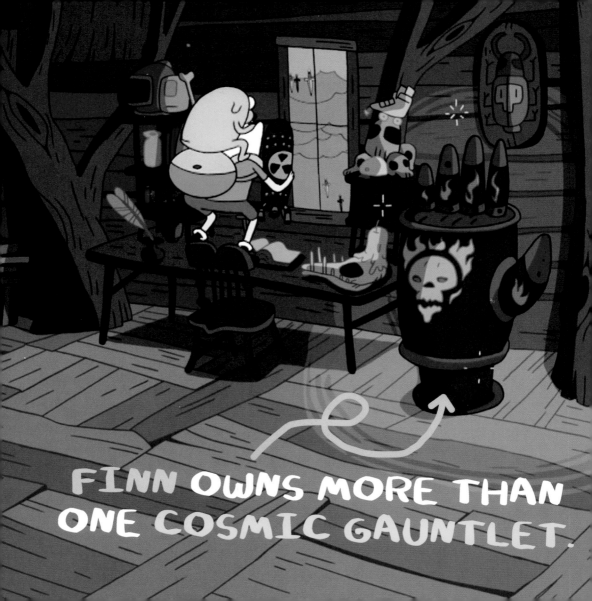

FINN OWNS MORE THAN ONE COSMIC GAUNTLET.

GUMBALL GUARDIANS ENFORCE THE KEEPING OF ROYAL PROMISES.

Jerky GRASS OGRES produce a gas called oboxygen. Gen.

You can play video games on BMO.

ONCE A YEAR FINN, JAKE, THE ICE KING, BMO, PRINCESS BUBBLEGUM, MARCELINE THE VAMPIRE QUEEN, CINNAMON BUN, PEPPERMINT BUTLER, PHIL, A CANDY CANE MAN, ONE OF THE GUMDROP GIRLS, LADY RAINICORN, LUMPY SPACE PRINCESS, THAT GUY, THE OTHER GUY, A PIG, TREE TRUNKS, A TWO-HEADED DUCK, THE OLD CRAZY TART TOTER, THE PUNCH BOWL, A BOOGER, AND GUNTER GET TOGETHER WEARING REALLY BIG SWEATERS AND WATCH VIDEOS ON THE FLOOR NEXT TO A FIRE.

INSIDE EVERY **APPLE**
THERE ARE FIVE SEED POCKETS.

BMO
CAN CHARGE CAMERAPHONES.

SPIDER MARRIAGE IS COMPLICATED.

ZANOITS KILL THOUSANDS OF PLANTOIDS EACH YEAR.

BABY WORMS ARE NOT BORN. They each hatch from a cocoon smaller than a grain of rice.

Traditional RAINICORN games include CAMELLADAPPAWOMAPFFFFT, which involves taking turns to create the best new colors.

DROP BALL IS A GAME WHERE YOU PICK UP A BALL WITH YOUR BUTT AND THEN DROP IT.

IN THE *BUG BATTLE* VIDEO GAME, YOU HAVE **TO KILL** BUGS.

BMO sets an alarm for Finn's Bath Time.

FINN'S BATH TIME

PHOTOGRAPHY IS ART.

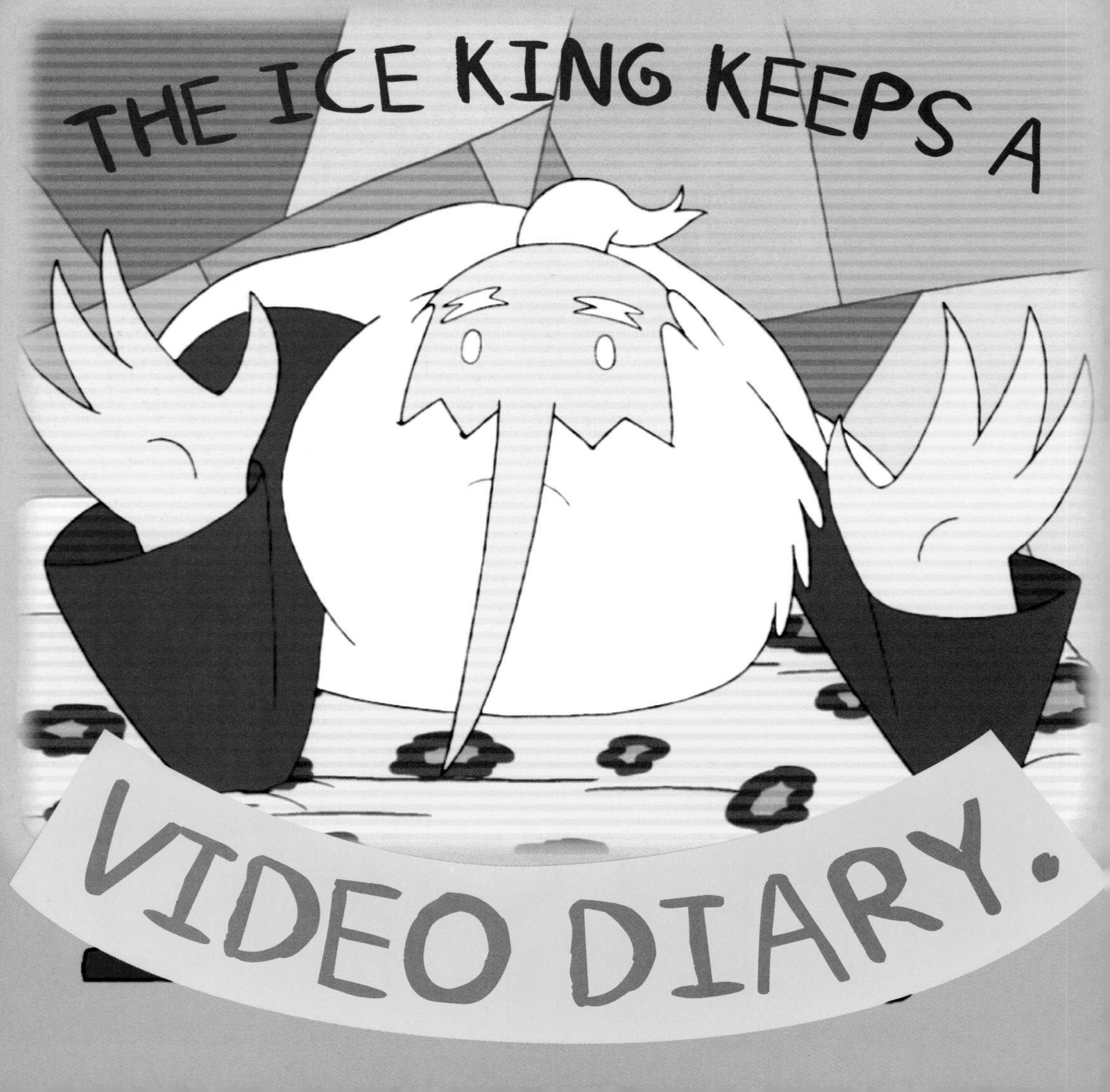
THE ICE KING KEEPS A
VIDEO DIARY.

MARCELINE

has been keeping a journal for 500 years.

THE MOLDOS LIKE TO EAT BOOKS, AND THEY ALSO LOVE THE TASTE OF JAKE'S FUR AND FINN'S SWEAT.

AN AWESOME
PRINCE IS THE
BEST KIND.

Card Wars is a fantasy card game that is supercomplicated and awesome.

BMO DOES NOT HAVE A SNOOZE BUTTON.

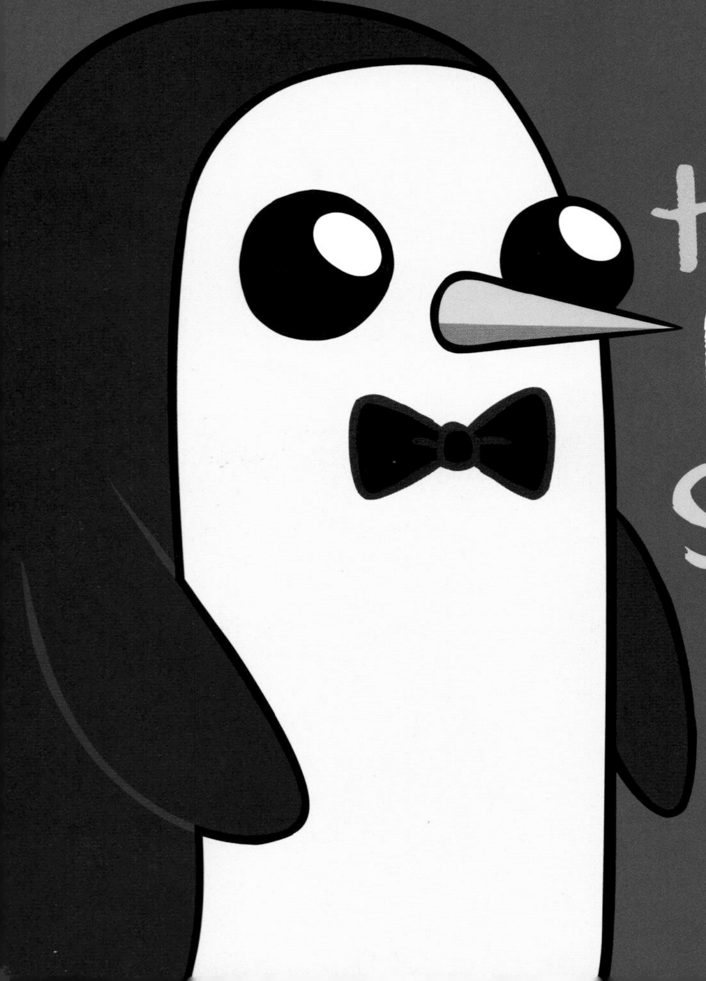

Gunter likes to eat the ICE KING'S SOCKS.

The **BANANA GUARDS** are the official royal guards of the **CANDY KINGDOM.**

THERE'S A MERMAID WHO LIVES IN THE RIVER OF JUNK— SHE'S PRETTY GROSS.

THE ARMOR OF ZELDRON WILL PROTECT YOU FROM EVIL, INCLUDING GHOSTS—BUT IT'S LADY ARMOR.